This Little Tiger book belongs to:

_____

_____

_____

For Tilly – M B

LITTLE TIGER PRESS
An imprint of Magi Publications
1 The Coda Centre, 189 Munster Road, London SW6 6AW
www.littletigerpress.com

First published in Great Britain 2012
This edition published 2012

Text and illustrations copyright © Matt Buckingham 2012
Matt Buckingham has asserted his right to be identified as the author
and illustrator of this work under the Copyright, Designs and Patents Act, 1988

A CIP catalogue record for this book is available
from the British Library

Bright Stanley
Double Trouble

Matt Buckingham

LITTLE TIGER PRESS
London

Far below the waves at the bottom of the sea lived a sparkly fish called Stanley.

His little cousin Dennis had come to stay, and he was very excited.

"I can't wait to play with you and your friends, Stanley!" said Dennis.

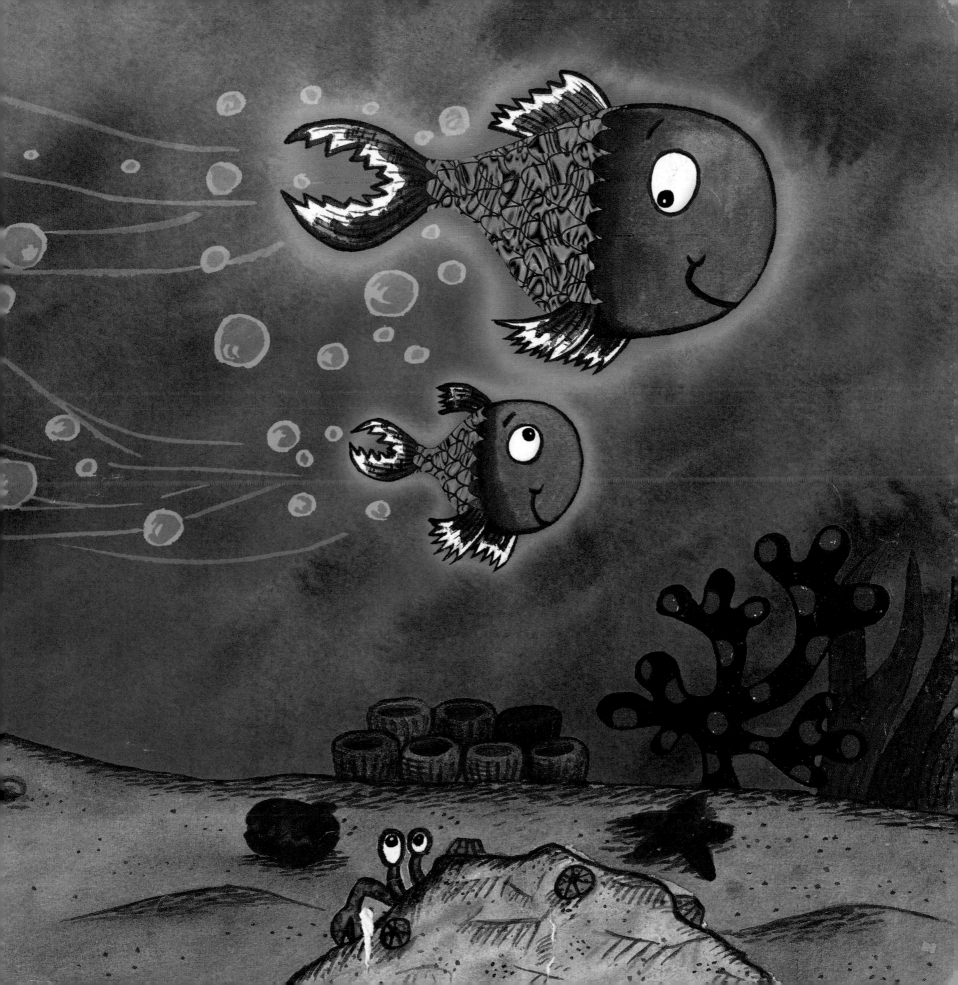

"Coo-ee! It's me-ee!" called Stanley to Percy, Turtle and Pufferfish. "This is my little cousin Dennis. I'm looking after him today."

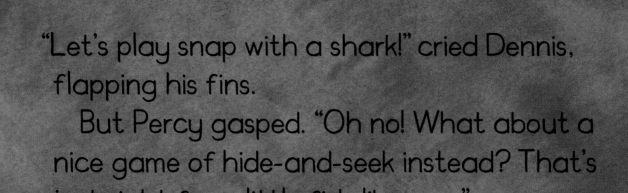

"Let's play snap with a shark!" cried Dennis, flapping his fins.

But Percy gasped. "Oh no! What about a nice game of hide-and-seek instead? That's just right for a little fish like you."

"OK," said Dennis. "Everyone hide
and I'll find you, even if you're in
a deep, dark cave. I'm not scared!"

"No peeping, Dennis," called Stanley.
Dennis counted slowly. ". . . 8, 9, 10.
Coming, ready or not!"

But the hiding places were far too easy
and not scary at all.

Dennis gave a big sigh. "Hide-and-seek
isn't much fun, after all," he said sadly.

"What shall we play next?" asked Pufferfish.

"I know – let's all arm-wrestle an octopus!" exclaimed Dennis.

"Or," smiled Stanley, "we could bounce on the sponges instead. Here, you have the little one, Dennis, so that you don't bounce too high and get dizzy."

But Dennis did the biggest bounce he could . . .

He shot off far into the sea! "Dennis, come back!" called Stanley. "I'm supposed to be looking after you."

"That was brilliant!" giggled Dennis.
"Oh, Dennis!" gasped Stanley. "I don't want
you getting into any more trouble. Let's play
I-Spy. That's a nice quiet game. You go first."

"OK," sighed Dennis. "If we have to.
I spy, with my little eye, something
beginning with . . . w."

"I know – a weed," said Percy.
"No," said Dennis.
"That's easy," boasted Turtle.
"Water!"
"Or is it a whelk?" asked Pufferfish.
"No," said Dennis.

"Oh, it's got to be a worm," said Stanley.

"No," giggled Dennis.

Everyone looked at each other.

"Well, what is it then?"

"...a whale!"

Dennis laughed.

"JUMPING JELLYFISH!" cried Stanley. "Swim for it!"

But it was too late. The whale opened his gigantic mouth and everyone was sucked inside.

It was very dark inside the
whale's mouth.
   "Oh, I'm scared," said Percy.
   "Me too," said Pufferfish and Turtle.
"Whatever are we going to do?"

PUFF!

POP!

But little Dennis wasn't scared.
"Don't worry, everyone. I know just
what to do!"

And using his feathery fins, Dennis
began to tickle. The whale began to
sniff and sniff until . . .

ACHOOOOOOO

The whale gave a huge sneeze.
Everyone was catapulted through
the water, in a whoosh of bubbles.
"Wheeee!" cried Dennis.

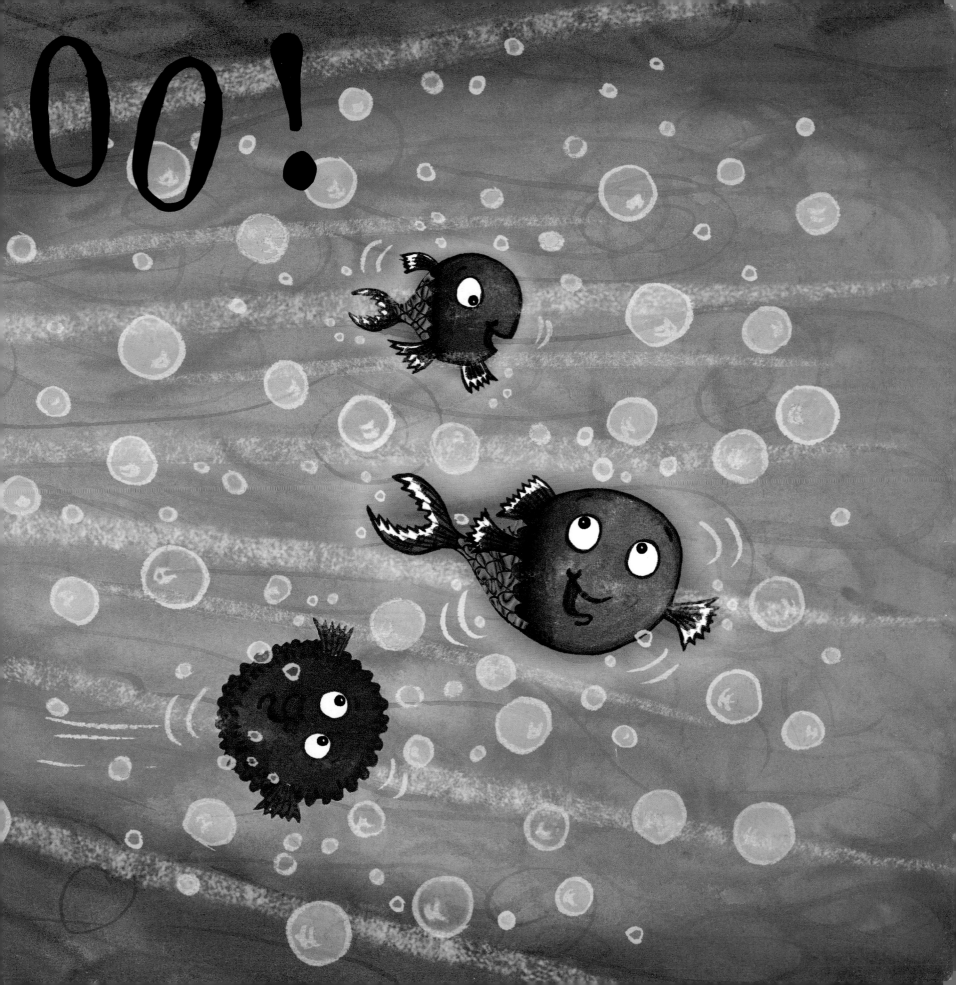

"That was the best game ever!"
laughed Dennis.
"Well done, Dennis," said Pufferfish.
"What a brave little fish you are!"

Stanley looked at his cousin and giggled. "I think *you* should be the one who looks after *us*, Dennis!"

Little Dennis gave a great big smile and the five friends swam off to play.

Make a **splash** with these fantastic books from Little Tiger Press!

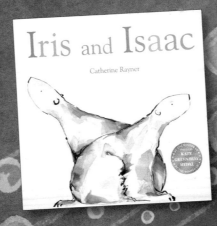

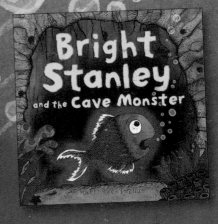

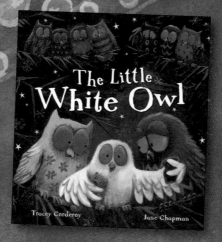

For information regarding any of the above titles or for our catalogue, please contact us:
Little Tiger Press, 1 The Coda Centre,
189 Munster Road, London SW6 6AW
Tel: 020 7385 6333 • Fax: 020 7385 7333
E-mail: info@littletiger.co.uk • www.littletigerpress.com